Willie Roy Dewberry's Panther

Willie Roy Dewberry's Panther

by Ben Douglas

Illustrated by Mary Lane Reed

Sontag Press
Madison, Mississippi

Copyright © 1996, by Ben Douglas

ISBN: 1-885483-01-5

Cover design by Carol Buchanan
Text design by Leslie Cummins

Published by:
Sontag Press
P.O. Box 1487
Madison, Mississippi 39130
800/497-3172

Distributed by Southern Publishers Group
1-800-628-0903

To
Paul, Troy, and J.B.
-B.D.

To
Steve
-M.R.

Chapter 1

Clang! Clang! Clang!

The ringing of the big school bell told the kids it was time for lunch. They stood and started for the door. Everyone stood except John, that is. He tried, but he tripped and fell to the floor.

Willie Roy Dewberry chuckled. Then he giggled. Finally, he howled with laughter. He had tied John's shoelaces together while John was hard at work on his math problems.

"What's the matter, John?" asked Willie Roy. "You got two left feet?" Willie Roy put his ankles together and hopped about. The kids laughed.

John struggled to bring his feet around in front of him. "Darn it!" he said through clenched teeth. His face turned red.

This was the latest of Willie Roy Dewberry's practical jokes. Willie Roy had scared John and Lucas — Lucas was John's little brother — by hitting the barn with a board while they were inside shelling corn. Once, he had tied John's and Lucas' clothes in knots while they were swimming in the creek.

Willie Roy had hidden their homework. He had

even tricked them into going on an errand that their mother hadn't sent them on.

Willie Roy Dewberry and John were the same age and in the same grade. They didn't look alike, though. Willie Roy had brown hair, brown eyes and a fat, round face. He was heavier than John but he wasn't as muscular, and he couldn't run as fast. John and Lucas saw Willie Roy almost every day, even at church on Sunday.

Willie Roy had two brothers and a sister who were very old. They were in high school. He also had a younger brother and a younger sister. Sometimes he pestered them. He had so much fun playing jokes on John and Lucas he wished he had started doing it long ago.

Willie Roy had been playing practical jokes on John and Lucas since the beginning of school. His practical jokes kept getting better and better.

John tugged at the knots in his shoelaces. "Willie Roy Dewberry," he said, "I'll get you for this." The kids watched him struggle with the shoelaces. "Darn it!" he said again.

"Oh, I'm so scared," said Willie Roy. He laughed so hard he could barely speak. The others laughed, too, as they went out the door.

As John sat on the wooden floor untying his shoe laces, the smell of the cleaning oil that had been used on the floor took his mind off food. He looked about. The heater in the corner of the room which contained a glowing fire during the winter was cold and empty. It was shaped like a large, black barrel, and seemed to be grinning at him.

The odor of the lunch being served drifted into the room, but John wasn't hungry. His mouth was dry and he felt hot. The kids in the lunch room sounded happy, like a flock of geese that had found some corn.

John stood and brushed the dust from his clothes. He walked into the large room where the kids were eating. Most of the time it was used as a lunch room, but sometimes it was used for special school programs.

The benches on which people sat during the school programs had been pushed aside to make room for the lunch tables. They would wait in neat rows until it was time for them to be used again.

The room was bright and open. Large windows let in light. Through the windows, and beyond the playground, pastures and woods could be seen. Several doors opened to the outside, as if they were inviting everyone to escape.

The sound of the forks and spoons on the plates grew louder as the kids finished eating. After lunch they went outside and played for a while, then classes began again. They played after lunch every day, but this was an especially good day. It was Friday.

"I'm glad it's Friday," mumbled John. "At least I won't have to put up with Willie Roy Dewberry this weekend. I'm going camping."

John had no way of knowing it would be a camping trip he would never forget.

Chapter 2

The leaves crunched beneath John's and Lucas' feet as they walked through the woods in search of a campsite. Nebo, their dog, followed. The camping gear was beginning to grow heavy on their shoulders.

"Do you want to pitch the tent here?" asked John. They were near the creek.

"Yeah, this is a good spot," said Lucas. The ground was flat and protected by a big tree. John and Lucas had camped here before. They dropped their gear and rolled out the tent.

Nebo wagged his tail and sniffed at the tent. "Move, Nebo," said John. "You're always underfoot." Nebo was a hound dog but it was hard to tell exactly what kind of hound. He was brown and black with some white showing here and there.

John and Lucas had walked from their house to the creek. They lived on a farm. John was in the sixth grade. Lucas was in the fourth. Both had light hair and lean, muscular bodies. They were of average height. By summer's end their skins would be brown and tough. Their feet would be tough, too. They always go barefoot all summer long.

"Why do they call these things pup tents?" asked Lucas.

"I guess they're about big enough for a dog to sleep in," said John. He and Lucas had their dog Nebo and some cats for pets. They also had a horse, cows, pigs, turkeys, and chickens on the farm. The horse was one of their prized possessions. John pointed toward a small bag. "Hand me those tent stakes," he said.

Lucas tossed the tent stakes to John. "I guess a dog could sleep in it if he's a little dog," said Lucas. Lucas talked a lot but most of the time John pretended not to notice. Lucas began unpacking the camping gear. "I like camping out," he said.

"Me, too. I'm not going to think about school, or anything. I'm going to go swimming and have a good time."

"I reckon it will be peaceful enough," said Lucas. "At least, Willie Roy Dewberry isn't here. . .I like playing with Willie Roy, but I'm getting kind of tired of his practical jokes."

"Me, too," said John. "His jokes are bad enough, but it's really not any fun when the kids at school laugh because they think Willie Roy is so clever."

"Yeah, even when he plays one of his dumb jokes on us somewhere besides school he can't wait to get back to school and tell everybody about it."

John didn't mind so much if the guys laughed — he could laugh at himself, sometimes — but his darkest secret was that he liked Nancy Rodgers. Who wouldn't? Nancy had thick blond curls and eyes as blue as a summer sky. When she smiled, dimples appeared in her cheeks and she flashed white teeth. It embarrassed John to think about her laughing at Willie Roy Dewberry's practical jokes.

John hadn't told Lucas about Nancy. Lucas wouldn't

understand, even though Nancy was perfect. Well, maybe not perfect. She was the youngest of six children and a little spoiled. And she kind of acted goofy when she saw things such as bugs, snakes, and mice, but most everyone liked her.

John hadn't told Nancy that he liked her, either, but he would. In the meantime, he wanted her to see he could take care of himself. He wanted her to see he could handle just about anything that came up, but Willie Roy Dewberry was causing problems. Willie Roy was making him look like a helpless little kid.

"You'd think Willie Roy would get tired of his dumb jokes," said Lucas.

"Maybe if we ignore him, he will quit." John knew he wouldn't but he was ready to change the subject.

John finished hammering the tent stakes into the ground and wiped his hands on his jeans. He and Lucas wore jeans every day, except Sunday. On Sunday they wore white shirts and khaki pants to the little country church.

"Naw, he won't quit," said Lucas. "Besides, ignoring Willie Roy is like trying to ignore a place that itches; the more you ignore it, the more it itches."

"Yeah, you're right. I know one thing, we have got to play a *real* practical joke on him. Like the biggest practical joke of all time. . .We'll embarrass him real good. . .Let him know how it feels."

That's what a cowboy would do, and John was going to be a cowboy when he grew up. Of all the adventure stories that he read he liked the ones about the wild west best of all. One day he would be a cowboy and have lots of horses and cows. Cowboys didn't put up with practical jokes.

"It would have to be one whopper of a joke to get Willie Roy's attention," said Lucas. Lucas hadn't thought about what he wanted to be when he grew up. Right now all he thought about was having fun. When he grew up, he might live in the jungle like Tarzan, or maybe drive a train. Either would be fun.

"Yeah, reckon it would have to be a whopper of a joke. . .We'll come up with something. . .We've got to. But I don't want to think about Willie Roy right now. I'll worry about him later."

"Want to go swimming?"

"Yeah, last one in is a rotten egg."

They ran for the creek.

The clear water in the tree-shaded creek never got warm, not even during the hot summer months. John and Lucas jumped in. *Chu-lug!* That was better than trying to get wet a little bit at a time. An instant later the water felt good. Trying to ease into cold water was a good way to freeze to death.

The water had a clean taste and smelled as if it had come from the very heart of nature. The sun shone down from a blue sky through a lot of thick, green leaves. It was almost summertime. There were only two more weeks of school. It didn't feel like summertime in the creek.

Nebo was the rotten egg. He ran to the edge of the water, stopped and drank. "Come on, Nebo, you chicken," called Lucas. "Come on, boy." Nebo plunged in.

John and Lucas and Nebo lost track of time. They swam until they were tired.

When John climbed out of the water, he looked at the western sky. "The sun is setting," he said.

"Let's get a camp fire going," said Lucas. "I'm hungry."

"Me, too," said John. "How about you, Nebo?" Nebo wagged his tail.

"Can't beat food that's cooked over a campfire," said Lucas.

14

"It's better than indoor food," said John. The food, the smell of the fire, and the warm glow of red coals made the campsite cozy.

John and Lucas would fall asleep to the sound of crickets, croaking frogs, and singing whippoorwills. Everything was perfect. It would be a peaceful night.

When they finished eating, they washed the dishes and packed things away. When Nebo finished eating, he wallowed out a bed for himself in a pile of leaves.

"Think Dad will come spend the night with us?" asked Lucas.

"Yeah, probably, after he milks the cows. . .Why? You scared?"

"Naw, I'm not scared. . .I heard there are panthers in these woods, though."

"There are no panthers in these woods," said John.

"I've heard that there are."

"If there are panthers in these woods, they are afraid of fire. . .and Nebo will bark at them."

"They ain't scared of Nebo."

"Tell you one thing," said John, "if you start talking about panthers and ghosts and such, you're going to talk yourself into being scared. . .I'm going to sleep."

"Aren't you going to stay up and wait for Dad?"

"No, you can stay up if you want to. . .Just watch out for the panthers."

"Real funny."

The night was dark and nearly silent. Suddenly, the crickets stopped chirping. Only the croaking of a lone bullfrog could be heard.

John and Lucas were spreading their blankets inside the tent when the bullfrog stopped croaking. It was unusual for the woods to be so quiet, so unusual John and Lucas stopped what they were doing and listened.

A twig snapped in the darkness. John and Lucas looked at each other. They didn't say anything. A moment later Lucas spoke in a loud whisper.

"Is that you, Dad?" he called. There was no answer. "Dad?"

"It's probably just the wind," said John.

"I don't know. . ."

A low growl came from Nebo's throat — a warning growl.

"John," whispered Lucas, "there's something, or someone, out there."

They saw a movement deep in the shadows.

Then they heard the scream.

Chapter 3

"AHHHH!"

Nebo sprang to life. "Ruff! Ruff! Ruff!," his deep, loud voice echoed through the darkness. The hair on his back stood up.

"AHHHH!"

"Yeeeooow!" yelled John and Lucas. They usually made the right decision in an emergency, and they made the right decision this time. They bolted from the tent and ran for their lives.

"AHHHH!"

"Yeeeooow! A ghost!" yelled Lucas. "A ghost!" Nebo was barking but the ghost came right on into the campsite. If the ghost wasn't afraid of Nebo, it must be an awfully fearsome ghost.

As they scrambled for the darkness of the woods, John tripped on one of the tent lines and jerked a stake out of the ground. The tent collapsed. He jumped up and ran.

"AHHHH!"

"Ruff, ruff." This time Nebo's voice wasn't as deep or as loud.

As John was running through the woods, he quickly

looked back at the campsite. There in the glow of the fire stood a ghost — a medium-sized ghost, to be sure, but a ghost. It was shaking, and jumping about the campsite. Its eerie shadow danced on the trees. Nebo was looking up at the ghost and wagging his tail. John stopped running.

"Lucas!" he shouted. "Wait a minute." John's breath came in short gasps. His heart still pounded against his chest, but it was beginning to beat more slowly. He wiped the sweat from his forehead. He balled his hands into fists and clenched his teeth.

"HA-HA-HA!" The voice of the "ghost" rang out through the woods. "HAR-HAR-HAR! What are you fraidycats running from?"

"Wouldn't you know it," said Lucas, "Willie Roy Dewberry."

"Willie Roy," said John, "I ought to. . ."

"It was a joke," said Willie Roy. He pulled the sheet from his head and stepped back. " You ain't been hurt. You're man enough to take a joke, ain't you?" He laughed nervously.

"Sometimes your jokes aren't funny."

"Yeah, they are. You're just embarrassed 'cause I'm gonna tell the kids at school." He laughed again.

"Willie Roy!"

"Just kidding, John. I'm just kidding. I ain't gonna tell nobody."

"Willie Roy," said Lucas, "one of these days you're going to get it."

"Get what, Little Brother?" asked Willie Roy. He knew Lucas didn't like being called "Little Brother," but he thought all the younger kids were scared of him.

Willie Roy wasn't afraid to speak up to Lucas. "You going to play a joke on ol' Willie Roy? You ain't got it in you. Even if you did," he said, pointing to his chest with his finger, "I could take it like a man. *I* wouldn't go running off through the woods like some scared little puppy."

"You wouldn't, huh?" asked John.

"Naw. Besides, I don't know anybody smart enough to play a joke on Willie Roy Dewberry." He chuckled, looked down his nose at Lucas and grinned.

John studied Willie Roy for a second. He smiled. "Willie Roy," he said. "I've got to hand it to you. You can come up with some good practical jokes. You got us good that time."

"You ain't mad?"

"Naw, We know it was all in fun."

"Yeah?"

"Yeah. . .Say. . .Why don't you spend the night with us? We have plenty to eat, and we'll make room for you in the tent. We'll go swimming tomorrow, have a good time."

Lucas started to protest. "John. . ."

"You're up to something," said Willie Roy. He looked at John, then at Lucas. He looked around the campsite. "You're up to something," he said again. "I know you are. You ain't wanting me to stay the night for no reason. You're still mad."

"No-o-o," said John. "I can take a joke."

"Well, I can't stay anyway. Mama told me to come straight home after I stopped and said 'Hi' to you."

"Some way to say 'Hi,'" said Lucas.

Willie Roy chuckled. "Little Brother, I was gonna say 'Hi' but you took off through the bushes so fast I didn't get a chance to. HAR, HAR, HAR!"

Willie Roy wasn't going to spend the night in the woods. He acted tough but he was afraid of his shadow and he was afraid someone would find out that he was afraid of his shadow. He would turn tail and run at the first sign of danger.

Willie Roy Dewberry was afraid of ghosts, monsters, black cats, and wild animals. He was afraid of witches, goblins, spooks, and Friday the thirteenth. He wouldn't walk under a ladder. He couldn't stand to see an empty rocking chair rocking. He was afraid it would attract ghosts.

Willie Roy was brave enough to scare John and Lucas because he knew ghosts and monsters didn't come out until after midnight. John and Lucas had a fire going and fires scared off ghosts and monsters and things. Besides, his house was close by and he could make a run for it if he had to.

"I've got to go now," said Willie Roy. He wadded up the sheet and tucked it under his arm. "Watch out for the ghosts and goblins. Hee, hee."

"And you watch out for panthers," said John.

"Huh?"

"Watch out for panthers. We heard one roar a little while ago."

"There ain't no panthers in these woods," said Willie Roy.

"Maybe not," said John.

Willie Roy mumbled a goodby and left. When he was out of sight of the camp fire he said to himself, "What if there *is* a panther in these woods?" He ran all the way home.

John and Lucas put their camp in order. Nebo went back to his bed in the leaves. John and Lucas fussed about Willie Roy. They got mad all over again. Then they tried to laugh about the trick he had played on them. There was no point in trying to forget it. They couldn't. One thing was certain: They had to come up with the best practical joke of all time to play on Willie Roy Dewberry if they had any hope of putting a stop to his foolishness. It had not been a peaceful night.

"Oh no!" moaned John.

"What?" asked Lucas.

"There's something we *have* to do first thing Monday morning, or else we're in big trouble."

Chapter 4

The rooster was still asleep on Monday morning when John shook Lucas. "Lucas, wake up!"

"Uh? What time is it?"

"Get up!"

"Why are you getting up so early?"

"So we can get our chores done. We've got to get to school before Willie Roy Dewberry does."

"How come?"

"I told you why already. We've got to tell everybody what happened at the creek. We'll pretend there wasn't much to it. We'll tell how we tried to get Willie Roy to spend the night. If he starts anything, we'll ask him if he was scared to spend the night with us."

"Who cares?"

"If Willie Roy gets to school before we do, there's no telling what he will say. He will probably say we jumped out of our skins and fainted and goodness knows what else."

"So what," said Lucas. "Everybody knows Willie Roy Dewberry tells tall tales."

Everyone knew, but that wasn't the point. John

didn't want Willie Roy to get away with telling tall tales when Nancy Rodgers was around to hear them. And John didn't want Willie Roy to enjoy his pranks too much. He would keep up the practical jokes as long as he was having fun.

John always looked on the bright side of things, but he was having a hard time seeing the bright side of this. He had to get to school before Willie Roy did. He also had to get his chores done. Chores came first.

Lucas looked on the bright side of things, too. "I'm not thinking about Willie Roy Dewberry," he said. Why should he worry his brain? Let John figure out something.

"Come on, let's get moving. You'll think differently when you wake up."

John knew that trying to rush chores was like trying to rush Christmas, but he tried, anyway. The more he rushed, the slower things went: The barn door was stuck. The cows didn't want to come out of the barn. The horse didn't want to go into the pasture. It seemed as if they knew he was in a rush, and they weren't going to do what he wanted them to do. Everything moved in slow motion.

When John and Lucas finally picked up their books and headed out the door for school, John said, "Hurry, maybe we can still make it."

"Wait a minute," said Lucas.

"Why?"

"I forgot something Mama told us to do. I'll be right back." Lucas ran to the kitchen. He was back in a second. "Mama wants us to drop off this butter at Miss Fay's on the way to school."

"Oh, no!"

What else is going to happen, thought John. Miss Fay is an old lady who lives alone. Why does she have to have butter today? She probably has plenty of butter. It doesn't matter. We have to drop off the butter even if Miss Fay does have butter, and even if Willie Roy Dewberry does beat us to school. Mama said so.

They ran most of the way to Miss Fay's. They left Miss Fay's and headed straight for school.

"Willie Roy has to walk to school, too," said Lucas. "If he is slow with his chores, he might not be there yet."

John and Lucas huffed and puffed their way along the road. "Willie Roy has caused so much trouble I'm never going to let him ride in my truck," said Lucas.

"You don't have a truck," said John. John wasn't in a mood to talk but he knew Lucas was going to clatter on about a truck that he didn't have, anyway.

"I'm going to have a great big red truck one of these days. . .when I get rich."

"Yeah, well, Willie Roy might not even be living here then."

"If he is, he ain't going to ride in my truck. . .You going to get a truck when you grow up?"

"No," said John. "I'm going to have a car, a green one without a top." John wondered how people ever got enough money to buy a car. All he had to his name was a pocket knife and a basketball. (He couldn't count things such as the farm animals and the camping stuff. They belonged to the whole family.) He was going to get a car one day, though. He wondered if Nancy Rodgers would like riding in a shiny green car. Was Nancy, at this very moment, listening to Willie Roy brag about his latest practical joke?

Through the trees John and Lucas saw the school. It was a white wooden building with a tin roof. The wavy window panes reflected the red of the early morning sun. No one was in front of the school. John and Lucas didn't expect there to be. Everyone would be on the playground behind the school.

"Hurry!" said John. "Maybe Willie Roy isn't there yet." Please! Please, don't let him be there.

John and Lucas ran to the rear of the school.

"Oh no!" said John. "I can't believe it!"

Chapter 5

"There was ol' John way up in a tree," said Willie Roy. "His hair was standing straight up. His eyes were as big as pie pans."

A group of kids had gathered around to hear Willie Roy's story. The more Willie Roy talked, the more they laughed. Willie Roy was enjoying himself.

"What was Lucas doing all this time?" someone asked.

"I heard Little Brother hit the creek. Splash! He was scared half to death."

"John must have been scared, too, if he climbed a tree."

"Yeah, he was scared, but he didn't exactly climb a tree," said Willie Roy. "There was a limb about ten feet off the ground. Ol' John jumped flat-footed up to that limb."

John stepped around the corner of the building. "I don't remember being up in a tree, Willie Roy." John looked about. Nancy Rodgers wasn't among the group gathered around Willie Roy. She was standing off to one side. But she could hear. John felt his heart drop to the center of his stomach. His face turned red.

Willie Roy was startled at the sound of John's voice.

He didn't know whether to smile, to be embarrassed, or to run. He would have his fun, but he sure didn't want to make John angry.

Willie Roy looked at John. John didn't appear angry, at least not angry enough to punch him in the nose.

Some of Willie Roy's courage returned. He said, "Well, it sure did look like you. I could have sworn it was you up in that tree. Sure wasn't a bunch of leaves up there a shakin' all by themselves. Hee, hee." The kids laughed with Willie Roy. John's face turned redder.

Willie Roy continued, "When I let out a yell, John and Little Brother scrambled outa there like their shirt tails were on fire."

"Don't call me 'Little Brother' or I'll. . ."

"You'll what, 'Little' . . ."

"Yeah, we were real scared, Willie Roy," John interrupted. "We knew who it was before you got that sheet off. . .Even ol' Nebo was standing there waggin' his tail at you. You didn't fool him with your dumb joke, either."

Willie Roy was not going to be outdone. "John and Lucas were running through the woods like a wild booger was after them."

"I thought you said I was in a tree," said John. He had Willie Roy now. Willie Roy had told the story two different ways. John smiled. He could take care of himself. He looked to see if Nancy Rodgers approved. Nancy wasn't there. John was disappointed.

Willie Roy wouldn't give up. "Well, uh, yeah. . .yeah," he said. "You ran through the woods 'fore you jumped up in a tree."

"Sure we did," said John. He turned to the kids. "You all know you can believe everything Willie Roy says." Doggone it! He had taken some of the sting out of Willie

Roy's practical joke and Nancy Rodgers wasn't there to hear him do it.

"Well, it's the truth. . .Admit it. You ran. . .I bet you couldn't go to sleep that night."

"N-o-o, I couldn't go to sleep," said John. "I tossed and turned about five seconds before I went to sleep."

John was tempted to walk away and ignore the whole thing. Let Willie Roy have his fun. He didn't care. He didn't care what anyone thought. Well, maybe he did care what Nancy Rodgers thought. "Willie Roy," he said, "you've got one coming. I'm going to get you good."

"Har, har, har." Willie Roy laughed. "You got to be joking. I ain't seen the person yet that could get Willie Roy Dewberry. You ain't as good at this as I am. . ."

Willie Roy turned to the kids. "Tell you what," he said, "I'll make ya'll a bet. I'll get a good one on John and Little Brother again before this week is out. . .Anybody want to bet?" The kids laughed.

"See, John," said Willie Roy, "there ain't no takers 'cause they know I can do it. I'm gonna do it anyway, though. You and Little Brother better watch out. I'll get you good before Friday."

"I'm so scared," said John. . . He started to walk away. "Who wants to play a quick game of basketball?" he asked.

John played basketball, but his heart wasn't in it. Willie Roy had gotten the best of him. John had tried to let the kids know Willie Roy was exaggerating, but they didn't care. They were too busy listening to Willie Roy's story. They were too busy laughing. And Nancy had left. She probably thought he was the biggest jerk in the whole school.

John kicked at the dirt. Darn that Willie Roy, he

thought. I ought to punch him in the nose. I'll bet that would stop his stupid practical jokes. I'd get in trouble if I did, though. And everybody would feel sorry for him. Nancy would probably think I was a bully. It doesn't matter. She probably thinks I'm a jerk, anyway. Let her think what she wants to think. I don't care. I don't care what any of them think.

Clang! Clang! Clang!

The school bell startled John. It was time for classes to begin. Everyone began walking toward the door. John kicked at the dirt again. "I'll fix that Willie Roy," he muttered. "I don't know how, but I'm going to play a practical joke on him he will never forget."

"Come on, John," said Willie Roy. "School is going to be fun today."

"How come?" asked John. He usually enjoyed school, but he didn't see how it could be fun today, not with Willie Roy talking about his practical jokes, and not with Nancy Rodgers thinking he was a fraidycat.

"We're going to practice for our spring program."

"Oh, I forgot," said John. How could he have forgotten? He had been looking forward to the spring program. Maybe he would get a chance to talk to Nancy while they practiced the program. He would tell her how he was going to get even with Willie Roy. He would have the last laugh after all.

When the kids were all seated at their desks, Miss Winn, their teacher, said she had an important announcement. The kids were excited. Miss Winn had promised to assign parts in the spring program.

"I hope I'm the Happy Sun," John whispered. "I've got to get that part." He would show Willie Roy Dewberry. Willie Roy would be jealous. It would make up for the trouble Willie Roy had caused.

John thought "Happy Sun" was a dumb name for a part. He would probably have to stand on stage dressed in some goofy costume and maybe wear some silly thing on his head, but he didn't care what kind of costume he had to wear. He didn't care if it was a dumb part, either, he still wanted it. He wanted to be near Nancy during the program. . ."I've got to get that part," he said again.

John crossed his fingers.

Chapter 6

Just last week Miss Winn told the class about the spring program. It would be about farmers and Mother Nature and the Happy Sun. The class would practice for two weeks. On the last day of school they would present the program. Everyone in the whole school would be there.

Each person in the class would have a part. There would be farm families and forest creatures in the program. Someone would play the part of the Happy Sun. The Happy Sun would shine on the farms and the forests. Of course, someone would be Mother Nature.

John knew Nancy Rodgers would be Mother Nature. Nancy was the prettiest girl in the school, maybe the prettiest girl in the whole world. Mother Nature and the Happy Sun would talk to the farm families and the forest creatures. Mother Nature and the Happy Sun would talk to each other a lot, too. John smiled.

John would have to learn a lot of lines if he got the part of the Happy Sun. He didn't care. It would be fun learning lines with Nancy. She would learn them quickly. She was a good student. She was going to be an English teacher one day.

It would be fun standing in the center of the stage with Nancy during the play and at the end of the play. Time passed quickly when John talked to Nancy. She liked all the good things. Nancy loved farm animals, she liked reading adventure stories, and she liked homemade ice cream. John's heart was set on getting that part.

"John," asked Miss Winn, "will you please play the part of the father of one of the farm families?"

John was stunned. He looked at Miss Winn as if he had not heard the question. He looked at his classmates. He opened his mouth but no words came out.

"John?" asked Miss Winn.

"Y. . .Yes, Ma'am?" John replied.

"Will you please play the part of the father of one of the farm families?"

"Y. . .Yes, Ma'am," replied John. Miss Winn was nice and John always tried to do what she wanted him to do. Besides, he didn't want to *ask* for the part of the Happy Sun. He didn't want to appear selfish.

"I think John will make a wonderful father, don't you class?" asked Miss Winn.

"Yes, Miss Winn," the class replied.

Miss Winn had a way of making everyone feel good about the part he or she was to play in the spring program. The part of the father of the farm family was a good part. It was one of the main parts, but it wasn't like playing the part of the Happy Sun and talking to Mother Nature.

"I don't believe it," John mumbled. "I didn't get the part."

Miss Winn continued to assign parts, but John wasn't listening. Every once in a while he would hear a squeal of delight or a cheer when a part was assigned, but he paid no attention to who got the part. He didn't hear anything until he heard Miss Winn mention Mother Nature.

"Whoever plays the part of Mother Nature will have to learn lots of lines," said Miss Winn. She seemed to be in deep thought as she looked at the class. Then she said, "Nancy, will you please play the part of Mother Nature?"

"Yes, Miss Winn," replied Nancy.

"I knew it," whispered John. "I knew it."

"That leaves one more part," said Miss Winn. "We need someone who will be a very good Happy Sun."

John had the urge to raise his hand and tell Miss Winn he wanted the part. He would be a great Happy Sun. Couldn't she see he would be the best Happy Sun there ever was? John looked around the room. Who would be the Happy Sun? Willie Roy Dewberry was smiling. No. No, it couldn't be. Not. . .

"Willie Roy," said Miss Winn, "will you please play the part of the Happy Sun?"

"Yessum, Miss Winn," replied Willie Roy, "I'll be the Happy Sun." Willie Roy was grinning from ear to ear when he looked at John.

John clenched his fist. He wanted to pound his desk. He wanted to punch Willie Roy in the nose. How could this have happened? How? How? How?

"And now, class," said Miss Winn, "would you like to begin practicing?"

"Yea-a-a!" everyone replied, everyone except John, that is.

"Okay," said Miss Winn, "Nancy, you come and stand here. . .Willie Roy, you come and stand beside Nancy, and. . ."

John didn't hear the rest of it. He stood where he was told. He did what he was told to do. He took the part Miss Winn gave him to learn. He would take it home and memorize it. He spent a lot of time thinking.

Sometimes he wished Dad would buy another farm

and move far away. But if Dad did that, John would miss all his friends. He would miss the school, the little country church, the swimming hole, and everything else.

By the end of the day John decided it didn't matter that Willie Roy would be the Happy Sun. Willie Roy would have to memorize a lot of lines. John wouldn't have to memorize many lines to be the father of the farm family. Besides, he could talk to Nancy Rodgers anytime, if he wanted to.

John thought about Willie Roy and his practical jokes. They were making his life miserable. Suddenly, a smile spread across his face. "I've got it!" he said. "I know how I can scare the living daylights out of Willie Roy Dewberry!"

Chapter 7

The sun shined warm on the freshly plowed corn-field. As John and Lucas covered seed with the soft earth, John thought about his plan. He would put a stop to Willie Roy Dewberry's practical jokes. He just needed to work out a few details.

"Does the seed die when it is planted?" asked Lucas.

"No, its life goes into the new plant," said John. It was hard to think about working out details with Lucas running his mouth.

"The thing I like best about spring is eating water-melons," said Lucas.

"We eat watermelons in the summertime."

"Well, that's what I like best," said Lucas.

"Maybe we ought to plant a lot of watermelons this year."

"Yeah."

Spring is a good time of the year. Old Bossy's new calf arrives in the spring. Baby chicks hatch, green grass grows in the pasture, the vegetables and the corn are planted. The trees begin to put on new leaves. Everything comes to life.

Lucas kicked at a clod of dirt. "The thing I like best

about spring is getting out of school," he said.

"I thought the thing you liked best was eating watermelons," said John. Would Lucas *ever* run out of things to say?

"You can't eat watermelons until you get out of school."

"You don't know what you like best about spring," said John.

"Do, too. The thing I really like best is getting to go barefoot."

"I thought the thing you liked best was getting out of school," said John.

"You don't get to go barefoot until you get out of school."

"You could run a person nuts," said John. "It's hard to think with you clattering away all the time. Don't you ever want to just think about things and not clatter?"

"What's there to think about?"

They had come to the end of a row. John and Lucas kept a jug of water there in the shade of a tree when they worked in the field. They stopped for a drink. John told Lucas about his plan for scaring the living daylights out of Willie Roy Dewberry.

"We'll catch a king snake and put him in the barn. They are harmless, but Willie Roy is afraid of any kind of snake. The next time he comes over to play we'll play in the barn. We'll 'accidently' lock him in the barn with the snake. That ought to teach him a lesson."

"Yeah, then we will tell everybody at school about it."

"I'll bet he won't scare us again," said John, "or embarrass us at school."

"Yeah, and I'll bet he won't call me 'Little Brother' again, either."

"We've got to find a king snake," said John.

"Uh oh," said Lucas. "I've just thought of something. We can't put a snake in the barn."

"Why not?"

"Mama is afraid of snakes, too, maybe more afraid of them than Willie Roy is. If she finds out we put a snake in the barn, we'll be in big trouble."

"We've *got* to," pleaded John.

"*You* do it then," said Lucas. "I ain't getting in trouble with Mama over a snake."

John thought about it for a while. Lucas was right. It was such a good plan, too. He couldn't put the snake in the barn. "Darn it!" he said. He would like to drop the snake into Willie Roy's overalls. "Darn it!" he said again.

"We'd better finish planting this corn," said Lucas.

"I reckon," said John.

"Why do we plant so much corn?" asked Lucas.

"Why do we plant so much corn!" yelled John. "Why do we plant so much corn! What kind of question is that? I'll tell you why we plant so much corn. *Everything* eats corn." He kicked at a clod of dirt. "The cows, the calves, the horse, the pigs, the turkeys, the ducks, and the chickens all eat corn."

"Even us," said Lucas. He smiled, as he often did when John was upset.

"Yes, even us!" yelled John. "We eat corn-on-the-cob, fried corn, stewed corn, corn bread, and corn fritters! We put corn in the soup! And we eat grits. . .they're made from corn, you know!"

"Yeah, I know."

"Well, don't ask any more dumb questions 'till we finish!"

"When we finish," said Lucas, "you're gonna have to go to the store and get a sack of flour."

"I ain't going to get no flour!" yelled John. "Who said I was going to get a sack of flour!"

"Mama said."

John kicked hard at a clod of dirt. "Ow!" he said. It hurt but he wasn't going to let on that it hurt. John didn't have much to say the rest of the afternoon.

After he and Lucas finished planting the corn, John set out for the little country store. He walked fast. If he hurried, he might get there and back before dark. Tomorrow was a school day and he had some homework to do.

It was dark when John returned. He put the sack of flour in the kitchen and went to his room to find his books.

"What took you so long?" asked Lucas.

"There were some men on the front porch of the store sitting and talking."

"So? There are always men on the front porch of the store sitting and talking."

"Yeah, but they were telling the funniest story I ever heard," said John. "They were telling about how this guy nearly scared somebody to death."

"How?"

"With this thing he built," said John. "I think we can build one. It will be a little something extra we can add to the big plans I have for Mr. Willie Roy Dewberry."

"What are we going to build?"

"I'll tell you, and I'll tell you something else. . .Willie Roy Dewberry better watch out. He's gonna be scared like he ain't never been scared before."

"How?" asked Lucas.

"First we have to get some things together. Then . . ."

Before John could tell Lucas about his plans, Mama called them to supper.

"Let's go eat," said John. "I'll tell you after supper."

Chapter 8

The next morning John and Lucas were in an un-usually good mood as they walked to school. They kicked a pine cone down the gravel road and threw rocks at the fence posts. "At last Willie Roy Dewberry is going to get what's coming to him," said Lucas.

"Yeah, he is" said John, "and he has been asking for it."

John and Lucas were usually the first of the kids to arrive at school but some of them were already there this morning. They were on the playground behind the school.

Willie Roy was there. He was in a good mood, too. He was holding a basketball. "Hey, John, do you want to be on my team?" he asked. Willie Roy played practical jokes on John but, when it came to basketball, he knew he had a better chance of winning if John was on his team.

"Yeah, I reckon," said John.

Willie Roy looked at Lucas. "What are you grin-ning at, Little Brother?" he asked.

"You won't be calling me 'Little Brother' much longer," said Lucas. John poked Lucas in the ribs with his elbow. He didn't want Lucas to give away their plan.

"What do you mean by that?" asked Willie Roy.

"Are you going to talk, or are you going to play ball?" asked John.

"I'm gonna play, but Little Brother is acting like Mr. Smarty Pants this morning."

"Willie Roy!" said John. "Are you gonna play, or not?"

"Okay, okay, I'm coming," said Willie Roy. He looked at Lucas. "You'd better not try anything with me, Little Brother," he said.

When the school bell rang, the kids quit their games and started toward their classrooms. John was lost in thought and didn't notice who was walking beside him until she spoke.

"Hi, John," said Nancy Rodgers.

"Oh, uh. . .Hi, Nancy. How's it going?"

"Okay. How are things going with you?"

"Good. Real good. . .Couldn't be better."

"Couldn't?" asked Nancy.

"Aw, well, maybe a little."

"I know what you mean. . .I just knew you were going to be the Happy Sun in the spring play. . .The other kids did, too."

"Yeah, thought maybe I might. . .but Willie Roy will do a good job."

"I suppose," said Nancy, "but Willie Roy is sort of—oh, I don't know quite how to say this—sort of childish."

"Maybe, but he will do fine." John didn't understand why he was defending Willie Roy. After all, it was Willie Roy who was embarrassing him and trying to make him look like a fraidycat.

"You would have done better," said Nancy. She and John talked until they were seated at their desks.

When the class practiced the play, John found himself daydreaming. Every time he saw Willie Roy standing beside Nancy he thought about how nice it would be if he was standing there.

To John's surprise Willie Roy had learned very few of his lines. John would have learned all the lines by now. Miss Winn would have been proud of him. More importantly, Nancy would have been proud of him.

There was one more week of school after this week. John wouldn't see Nancy during the summer, except at church on Sunday. He had to stop Willie Roy's practical jokes within the next few days, but he couldn't do it in a way that would make him look like a little kid. Nancy wouldn't approve if he acted like a little kid.

He knew one thing: He had to do something now or it would be too late. . .if it wasn't too late already.

I'm going to build that contraption this afternoon or bust, he thought. He did, but he had no way of knowing Willie Roy Dewberry had plans of his own.

Chapter 9

That same afternoon Willie Roy Dewberry went to the pile of junk behind his barn and began poking through it. He was excited. Sam, his dog, stood nearby watching. Willie Roy talked to Sam while he worked.

"Dog," he said, "I have played some good tricks on John and Little Brother, but they ain't seen nothing yet. This is going to be the best trick anybody ever played on anybody." Sam wagged his tail.

Willie Roy threw some junk aside. "It's a good thing Mama sent me to the store last night. If she hadn't, I never would have heard about this."

Willie Roy found an old bucket. Most of the bottom was missing. It was just what he needed. "Matter of fact," he said, "those two fraidycats were about to catch on to all my tricks. . .That was bad for me, 'cause I'd told the kids at school I was gonna get John and Little Brother real good again this week."

Willie Roy picked up the bucket and walked into the barn. Sam followed. Willie Roy was still talking to Sam. "I got 'em good at the creek with my ghost trick, but I'd better not borrow any more of Mama's sheets. I'd be in big trouble if she found out. . .Besides, this will be ten times better than that ghost trick."

Willie Roy cut the remainder of the bottom out of the bucket. He searched through the barn and found an old piece of rawhide. It wasn't easy, but he finally managed to tie the rawhide over the end of the bucket.

"Dog," he said, "this would make a pretty good drum." Willie Roy punched a small hole in the middle of the rawhide. He cut a strip of rawhide and passed it through the hole. He tied a knot in one end so it wouldn't go all the way through.

Willie Roy now had a gadget that looked like a drum with one side missing, but with a rawhide tail dangling from the other side. It was perfect. "Dog," he said, "do you know what this thing is supposed to do?" Sam wagged his tail. "It's supposed to roar like a panther. . .I think I'll give it a try."

Willie Roy walked outside. The mule was nearby, and some chickens were scratching around in the dirt. "Let's see if the mule and the chickens think this thing sounds like a panther," he said. He grasped the rawhide strip near the bottom of the bucket. He held firmly to the strip and slid his hand down it.

The jerky movements his hand made while sliding along the rawhide strip caused a sound to come from the bucket, "Ou-ou-ou-ou-a-ah!"

Willie Roy's panther worked just as he had hoped it would. He tried it again. It worked even better this time. "OU-OU-OU-OU-A-AH!" it roared. The noise sounded so much like a real panther it scared every creature near the barn.

"Hee haw! Hee haw!" the mule brayed. He began running in circles and looking for a way to get over the fence to get away from the terrible critter that was roaring at him.

The chickens were squawking. Sam began howling like crazy. He barked and growled at the awful thing Willie Roy was holding. As Willie Roy was running to the mule to calm him, he saw Curtis, his big tomcat, scamper up a tree.

"Whoa, Cooksie!" he yelled to the mule. "Whoa! Whoa, boy! We're both going to be in trouble if you break through the fence. Whoa, Cooksie." Then Willie Roy spoke gently to the mule. "Whoa."

Cooksie looked at Willie Roy with large eyes that were rimmed with white. Finally, he settled down. Willie Roy managed to get Sam to stop growling. "You can come down out of the tree now, Curtis," he said to the cat, but Curtis was a smart cat. He wasn't about to come down out of the tree.

Willie Roy was proud of his panther. He had nearly gotten into trouble with it, but he was so excited his heart was pounding. He would scare John and Lucas, and their dogs and cats, and ducks, and turkeys, and everything else on their farm.

"Dog, I'm going to enjoy this. I'm going to have John and Little Brother begging for mercy." Sam looked at Willie Roy, but he wasn't wagging his tail. "Then they'll be begging me not to tell everyone at school. . .I will, though. The kids will be laughing so hard they'll be rolling on the ground. They'll know that Willie Roy Dewberry is the king of practical jokers. He's better than anybody in the whole world."

Willie Roy picked up his panther. "Dog," he said, "you had better stay home. This might be too scary for you. Hee, hee, hee. This is as good a time as any to scare the living daylights out of those two little corncobs. . .I know where those fraidycats are, too. They had to work in the garden today. . .I'll just sneak through the woods and let 'em have it."

Willie Roy stepped into the woods.

The woods were as cool as spring water. Large trees were everywhere, and smaller ones were scattered between them. The trees shaded the ground and kept it cool. New leaves were growing but the old leaves of winter still crunched under Willie Roy's feet.

The smell of the old leaves, the new leaves, and the blossoms in the woods was like smelling winter, spring, and summer all at once. Broken limbs had fallen and were lying about. If a limb didn't move, it was a limb. If it moved, it was a snake.

The bushes brushed against Willie Roy's arms and legs, as if they wanted him to know they were there. There were some black stumps in the woods. They looked like bears, but there were no bears in the woods. At least, he didn't think there were any bears in the woods.

The chirping of the birds and the buzzing of insects made the woods seem like a real jungle. Tarzan probably heard the same sounds in his jungle. Willie Roy could have pretended he was in Tarzan's jungle if he hadn't heard a cow bell in the distance.

The woods were peaceful enough, but Willie Roy had to watch out for briars and snakes. There was some danger, even in peaceful woods. Willie Roy was so excited he didn't stop to think about danger that might come his way.

"When I finish with those two little corncobs, they'll be so embarrassed they'll be begging their mama and papa to move to another country," he said.

Chapter 10

John and Lucas were in the vegetable garden. John was working. Lucas was working and talking. "Are you sure we can scare Willie Roy?" he asked.

"Yeah," said John. "I've told you a hundred times that the next time we catch him in the woods we'll scare him half to death."

"How are we going to get him to go in the woods?"

"I've told you that a hundred times, too. The next time he comes over to play we will play in the woods. You know what to do then?"

"Yeah."

"So don't ask me a hundred more times, okay?"

"I won't ask you that," said Lucas.

"Don't ask me *anything*."

"Okay, I won't ask you anything. . . Do you know what I like best about spring?"

"I thought you weren't going to ask me anything!" said John.

"I didn't ask you anything about Willie Roy," said Lucas, "I just asked if you know what I like best about spring."

"What? For goodness sake, *what* do you like best

about spring?"

"Summer comes next," said Lucas. "It's my favorite time of the year."

"I thought winter was your favorite time of the year."

"It is," said Lucas.

"Then you said spring is your favorite time of the year."

"It is."

"Now you're telling me summer is your favorite time of the year."

"It is," said Lucas.

"What about fall?"

"It's my favorite time of the year, too."

"Spring, summer, fall, winter — they can't *all* be your favorite time of the year," said John. Lucas could worry the horns off a brass billy goat.

"Maybe they can't all be *your* favorite time of the year, but they are *my* favorite time of the year."

"Look," said John, "we can finish this a lot faster if we work instead of talk."

"I can work and talk."

"It's a good thing," muttered John.

John kept right on working. Lucas kept right on working and talking. They both stopped when they heard a roar far off in the woods. They listened for another.

"That sounded like some kind of big cat," said John, "maybe a panther."

"Yeah, it did," said Lucas. He pointed toward the woods. "It sounded like it came from that direction."

"Do you know what I think?" asked John.

"Yeah, I'm thinking the same thing."

"You know what to do, don't you?" asked John.

"Yeah," said Lucas. "I'll be right back." He ran toward the barn.

Chapter 11

Willie Roy Dewberry was still a half mile from John's and Lucas' house when he stopped again. "I think I'll just give this ol' panther's tail another little stroke," he said. He was talking to himself, partly to keep from being afraid, and partly because he talked to himself when he was alone. "Then I'll do it again when I get closer. That way they'll think the panther is stalking them. They'll think he's going to get them, for sure."

Willie Roy was so proud of himself. He dragged his hand down the strip of rawhide. "OU-OU-OU-OU-A-AH!" roared the panther.

"Way to go, panther. . .John's and Little Brother's eyes are as big as saucers right now. They're shaking from head to toe. . .but just wait 'til we get up close and you let out a roar. They'll run straight for the house and hide under the bed. I wish I had a Kodak so I could take their picture. Boy! It would be fun to show that at school."

Willie Roy walked a little further. "Hee, hee, hee" he chuckled, "you're doing just fine, ol' panther." He patted his panther. "Why don't we give those fraidycats another little roar?"

Willie Roy drew his hand down the strip of rawhide. "OU-OU-OU-OU-A-AH!" roared the panther. Willie Roy laughed out loud. "I wish I could see those two little corncobs. I'll bet their eyes are big as two fried eggs in a skillet."

Willie Roy started to move even closer when from somewhere deep in the woods he heard, "OU-OU-OU-OU-A-AH!" He froze.

"Good golly! What was that?" he whispered. "Must be an echo."

Willie Roy was still trying to figure out what was going on when he heard it again, "OU-OU-OU-OU-A-AH!" This time the roar was louder, and from a different direction.

"That was no echo. That came from a living, breathing, walking-around critter." Willie Roy's mouth suddenly became dry. His heart thumped against his chest wall. He began to sweat.

"Good golly!" he said again. "It's an honest to goodness panther. He heard my panther roar and now he's coming to find me. That was a real man-eating panther I heard. He will eat me alive. I had better get out of here!" He threw down his panther and turned to run home.

Chapter 12

"OU-OU-OU-OU-A-AH!" came the roar from deep in the woods.

"Y-e-e-e-e-o-o-o-o-w!" screamed Willie Roy. "Help! Mama!" The panther was between Willie Roy and his house. If he tried to run home, he would run into the panther. He would have to run the other way. "Help! Mama! Help!"

Willie Roy began running through the woods. The briars and tree branches scratched his hands and face. John's and Lucas' house was maybe a quarter of a mile away. He had to get there and lock himself in the barn before the panther caught him.

"OU-OU-OU-OU-A-AH!"

"Y-e-e-e-e-o-o-o-o-w! He's closer! He's coming! He's coming! . . .Help! There's a panther on the loose!"

Sweat rolled off Willie Roy's face. His heart raced. He huffed and puffed as he ran, first up a hill, then down one. He made so much noise as he ran across the dry leaves he sounded like a large animal running through the woods.

Willie Roy came to a creek. "Wait! The creek is not supposed to be here. I crossed the creek already. . .Or I thought I did. . .Maybe I didn't. . .I must be turned around. I've got to go the other way! Help! Mama! Help!"

"OU-OU-OU-OU-A-AH!" The panther was behind Willie Roy.

Willie Roy didn't hesitate. He might be going the wrong way, but he didn't care. He splashed across the creek. Now his overalls were wet.

Willie Roy had a sudden glimmer of hope. "Maybe it's a good thing I crossed the creek," he said. There was no one to talk to, but by talking he could pretend someone was listening. "Cats don't like water. Maybe panthers don't, either. I'll get away from him while he is trying to decide whether or not to cross the creek."

"OU-OU-OU-OU-A-AH!"

Willie Roy dashed through the woods. His feet were pounding the leaves again. But above the noise of his running, and his hard panting, he heard a *swish, swish, swish*.

"O-o-oh n-o-o!" cried Willie Roy. Tears streamed down his face. "I can hear his feet on the leaves! He's gonna get me! He's gonna get me! Oh, *please* don't let me be eaten alive! Help, somebody! Help!"

Willie Roy was so frightened he forgot that wet overalls make a *swish, swish, swish* sound when you walk or run in them. Willie Roy ran harder. He could still hear the *swish, swish, swish* sound.

"OU-OU-OU-OU-A-AH!"

Willie Roy ran down a hill, crossed a stream, and collapsed at the end of a huge hollow log. "Maybe I've lost him. . .Maybe he won't cross a creek and a stream. No, I haven't lost him. He's still on my trail. I know one thing, if I ever get out of this alive, I'm *never* going to play jokes on anyone ever again. It was dumb, dumb, dumb to play jokes on anybody. John and Lucas are my best friends. Why did I ever play jokes on them? I wish they were here. John would know what to do."

Willie Roy lay panting. "I can't run anymore. He's gonna get me. . ."

Chapter 13

"I can't run anymore," Willie Roy repeated as he lay on the ground in front of the huge hollow log. He thought about hiding in the log. No, that wouldn't work. The panther could still get him. Hiding would do no good. A panther could follow his trail, could smell him even if he was hidden.

Willie Roy looked into the hollow log, anyway. He was not prepared for what he would see. He nearly fainted when he saw a large ball of fur. Two beady eyes stared at him from inside the log. When Willie Roy screamed, it scared the raccoon. Willie Roy discovered he *could* run some more.

"Y-e-e-e-e-o-o-o-o-w! It's a bear! It's a man-eating grizzly bear! Run for your lives! Y-e-e-e-e-o-o-o-o-w!"

Willie Roy flew through the woods. "Help! Mama!" he screamed. Tears began to roll down his cheeks again.

Willie Roy ran faster than he had ever run. Briars and branches scratched his hands and face again. He was dirty and tired. He smelled the dead leaves that clung to his clothes and he could still feel his heart pounding. His mouth was dry and tasted of copper. He wiped sweat from his eyes. Willie Roy pushed his hair out of his face. It was wet. He had run so hard he was dizzy. He stopped. This time he really couldn't run anymore.

"OU-OU-OU-OU-A-AH!"

He could run some more. He bounded on through the woods. A log lay across his path. He leaped upon it, paused, and was about to jump down on the other side when he heard a voice. Or he *thought* he heard a voice. Was he hearing things? He tried to listen hard, but all he could hear was his own heavy breathing. Would he soon begin seeing things, too?

He heard the voice again. Loudly and slowly someone yelled, "Wi-l-l-ie R-o-o-y."

Someone was calling his name. No, that couldn't be. Was he going crazy? No one knew he was in the woods. He listened. He wanted to hear the voice again. He would run toward whoever was calling him. Maybe they could help him get away from the panther. On the other hand, if he was going crazy, he didn't want to hear the voice again.

Willie Roy ran toward where he thought the person might be. If it was a real person and that person knew *he* was in the woods, then that person must also know a panther was in the woods. Willie Roy would have to run to whoever was calling him. Nobody would be fool enough to come into the woods as long as the panther was there. How foolish he had been to call up a panther.

"OU-OU-OU-OU-A-AH!" The panther was close now, too close for him to escape. How terribly this was all going to end! Maybe the person who was calling out to him would organize a search party.

The men of the community would come looking for him. They would have dogs who could trail things. They would search late into the night with flashlights. It would be too late. He would be dead before they got to him. But maybe they would get to him before the panther dragged his body deep into the swamp.

At least there would be a proper funeral at the church. That's all he could hope for now. He cried when he thought of his own funeral. The preacher would be standing behind the pulpit. Everyone in the community would be there.

My family will be sitting down front, he thought. Mama and Papa will be there. My brother and sister who are grown and in high school will be there. Everyone will be crying, even my little brother and little sister. If I ever had another chance, I would never pester them again.

John and Lucas will be at the funeral, dressed in their white shirts and khaki pants. They will miss me, even if I did play practical jokes on them. If I had it to do over again, I wouldn't, but they will never know that.

Uncle Simpson and Aunt Dilly who live in the city will come to the funeral. Uncle Simpson will wear his black high-top shoes and Aunt Dilly will wear her big hat. No one sitting behind her will be able to see the front of the church.

They'll carry me from the church to the graveyard. There will be a green tent over a big hole in the ground. A pile of red dirt will be beside the hole. The preacher will sprinkle some dirt on my casket and say some words. Then everybody will go home and milk the cows and feed the hogs.

They'll probably put my picture in the county paper. The headlines will say WILLIE ROY DEWBERRY EATEN BY PANTHER. It's awful. The most exciting thing I ever did in my whole life was get eaten by a panther.

Willie Roy saw a thicket of bushes up ahead. There appeared to be an open space — a field, perhaps — beyond the bushes. If he could make it to the field, or pasture, or whatever it was, maybe the panther wouldn't follow him out into the open. It was his only chance.

He ran for the bushes.

Chapter 14

John was still working in the vegetable garden, placing sticks beside young tomato plants and loosely tying the plants to the sticks so they would grow tall and straight. He could hear Willie Roy Dewberry yelling, but he kept right on working.

John could also hear the panther that was chasing Willie Roy, "OU-OU-OU-OU-A-AH!"

John tied a tomato plant to a stick, stood and called, "W-i-l-l-i-e R-o-o-y!"

There was a thicket of bushes between the garden where John was working and the nearby woods. Suddenly Willie Roy burst through the bushes and saw John calmly working in the garden.

"Hi, Willie Roy," said John. "What have you been up to?"

Willie Roy was stunned and gasping for breath. His face and hands were scratched. Tears streaked the dirt on his face. He was covered with bits of leaves and twigs. Dirt clung to his skin and to his wet overalls. He was sweating like he had been working in the hot sun.

Willie Roy's mouth dropped open and his eyes widened. John must have heard the panther, but he didn't look scared. Willie Roy quickly recovered.

"John!" he shouted. "John! There's a panther out there! He's been chasing me. . .and I ran across a *bear*, and. . .and we had better run! John! We had better run. We gotta lock ourselves in the barn!"

"Whoa, Willie Roy," said John, "how do you know there's a panther in the woods?"

"Well, you see, I made this thing that will roar like a panther, and. . ."

"And you were gonna scare us with it."

"No, no. . .I mean. . .yeah, I was but not anymore. I'm never gonna scare anybody else again. I'm never gonna play a joke on nobody."

"Never?" asked John.

"Never. Anyway, I called up a panther."

"Aw, Willie Roy," said John, "I don't think there's a panther in the woods."

"Yes, there is!" shouted Willie Roy. He grabbed John's arm and began pulling him toward the barn. "We'd better get out of here! I'm telling you he's gonna get us."

"OU-OU-OU-OU-A-AH!" The panther was not a stone's throw away when it roared.

"AH-H-H-H-H!" screamed Willie Roy. "He's right behind those bushes." Willie Roy dropped John's arm and fled.

"Help! Mama!" he screamed. He ran to the garden fence, jumped it and ran to the barn.

It was quiet for a time. A few minutes later Lucas walked from the woods. "Where's Willie Roy?" he asked.

"He's locked himself in the barn," said John, as he reached to tie another tomato plant to its stake.

Lucas cradled a bucket in his arm. One end of the bucket was covered with a piece of rawhide, and a strip of rawhide dangled from its center. The hand he had been dragging down the rawhide strip was beginning to get sore.

"Do you think I ought to stroke this ol' panther one more time?" asked Lucas.

"Naw," replied John, "let the panther rest. He must be tired. Matter of fact, let's hide him before Willie Roy comes out of the barn."

"Good idea," said Lucas, "I'll put him here under these bushes. . .You never know when we might need him again."

"That's right," said John.

"Do you think we ought to go get Willie Roy out of the barn, or just let him sit there for a while?"

"Let's let him sit there a while," said John. "He needs some time to do some thinking."

"You think we ought to leave him in the barn until we finish with these tomato plants?"

"Let's leave him in the barn until he decides to come out," said John.

Lucas laughed. "He might never come out."

"Oh, yeah he will," said John, "he will be coming out any minute now."

They heard Willie Roy Dewberry scream.

Chapter 15

"Y-e-e-e-e-o-o-o-o-w!" screamed Willie Roy. "H-e-l-l-p! M-a-a-ma!"

Blam! Blam!

"Sounds like Willie Roy is trying to tear down the barn," said Lucas. "Wonder what's wrong?"

"Maybe Willie Roy doesn't like sharing the barn with a king snake."

"A snake!" said Lucas. "But. . .but. . ."

"I found this little ol' king snake yesterday and I just couldn't resist the temptation. I put him in the barn. Sounds like Willie Roy has found him."

"Y-e-e-e-e-o-o-o-o-w!"

Blam! Blam!

"Yeah, he's found him all right," said Lucas. "You might have gotten in trouble, though."

"I might have, but I didn't. I knew Willie Roy would come over to play in a day or so. I figured it was worth taking the risk."

Blam! Blam!

"H-e-e-l-l-p!"

"Why doesn't Willie Roy just open the barn door?" asked Lucas.

"He's too excited, or maybe the snake is between him and the door. . .Sounds like he's trying to tear out the back of the barn."

"You think we ought to let him out?" asked Lucas.

"Yeah, I reckon. I think Willie Roy has about enjoyed all of this practical joke he can enjoy."

When John opened the barn door, the snake scurried away to hide under some corn.

"A snake!" yelled Willie Roy. "A man-eating boa constrictor."

As Willie Roy ran out the door, John grabbed him. If he hadn't grabbed Willie Roy, he might have run to the next county. "Whoa, Willie Roy," said John. "What's wrong?"

"A snake," yelled Willie Roy as he struggled to free himself from John's grasp. "He almost got me!"

John and Lucas began laughing.

"What?" asked Willie Roy. "What. . ."

John and Lucas continued to laugh. They laughed until their sides hurt. They told Willie Roy about the snake.

"You know," said John, "practical jokes are fun. I think we're going to have to do this more often."

"Yeah," said Lucas, "hearing Willie Roy yelling and calling for his mama was the funniest thing I've ever heard. I can't wait to tell the kids at school about it."

"I. . .I don't think it was too doggone funny," said Willie Roy. "I could have gotten hurt, you know."

"Yeah, we could have gotten hurt running through the woods in the middle of the night," said Lucas.

"Aw, Little Brother, that was different," said Willie Roy.

"Don't call me 'Little Brother.'"

Willie Roy started to reply, "Yeah, well, uh. . ." Then he remembered the panther. "Ya'll hear that panther?" he asked. He looked around nervously.

"Yeah," said John. "The panther's gone."

"Are you sure?" asked Willie Roy.

"We're sure."

"How do you know?"

John and Lucas looked at each other and grinned. "We heard him roar way over yonder," said John. "He must have been a mile away when we heard him. He's probably back in the swamp by now."

"Willie Roy," said Lucas, "let's go find your noise-maker. We can have fun with that thing. We can scare a lot of people."

"Ain't never going back in those woods, and I ain't ever gonna need that noisemaker," said Willie Roy, "and I ain't ever gonna fool with playing no more jokes on no-body."

"Never?" asked John.

"Never," replied Willie Roy. "They can backfire on you. . .Say, you ain't gonna tell anybody at school about this, are you?"

"Depends," said John.

"On what?"

"On whether or not you ever play a practical joke on us again."

"Oh, I won't," said Willie Roy. "You don't ever have to worry about that."

"And it depends on whether or not you ever call me 'Little Brother' again," said Lucas.

"N-o-o," said Willie Roy, "You don't have to worry about that, either. I wouldn't even *think* about calling you that. Just don't tell nobody at school about it." Willie Roy had a sheepish grin on his face. He looked as if he had lost his appetite for practical jokes.

"We'll see," said John.

"Yeah, we'll see," said Lucas.

Chapter 16

When the students were all seated at their desks, Miss Winn said, "I have an announcement. There's going to be a small change in our spring program. Willie Roy wants another part. He has been very busy on the farm and he hasn't had time to study his lines. That's okay but that means we need someone to play the part of the Happy Sun."

"I was going to ask for volunteers," Miss Winn continued, "but someone suggested that John would be good for the part, and I think he will, don't you, class?"

"Yes, Miss Winn," the class replied.

"John," said Miss Winn, "will you please play the part of the Happy Sun?"

"Oh, yes, Ma'am," replied John.

"Do you think you could memorize the lines in time? As you know, we only have one more week to practice."

"Oh, yes, Ma'am I can. I know most of the lines already."

"Willie Roy," asked Miss Winn, "will you play the part of the father of the farm family?"

"Yessum," replied Willie Roy.

"Do you think you can memorize the lines in time?"

"Yessum," replied Willie Roy. "John said he'd help me if I needed some help."

"Good!" said Miss Winn. "Let's practice."

As John and Lucas were walking home from school that afternoon, Lucas said, "I heard you got another part in the play."

"Yeah, how did you know?"

"Willie Roy told me," said Lucas.

"Yeah?"

"Yeah, Willie Roy is okay. He doesn't call me 'Little Brother' anymore. He's coming over Sunday to play."

"Good," said John.

"Willie Roy said you like Nancy Rodgers. He said she's your girlfriend."

"What does Willie Roy know?"

"I saw Nancy talking to you after school," said Lucas. Then, using his best imitation of a girl's voice, he said, "I heard her say, 'See you Sunday, John.'"

While John was trying to decide whether to clobber Lucas or ignore him, Lucas trotted down the road ahead of John. When he was some distance away, he called, in a teasing voice, "John and Nancy sitting in a tree K-I-S-S-I-N-G. . . ."

"Why, you. . ." said John. "When I catch you, I'm going to throw you in the creek with your clothes on."

Lucas began laughing. He turned and ran.